Wish Upon a Superstar

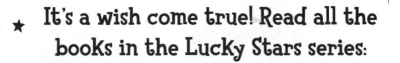

It's a wish come true! Read all the
books in the Lucky Stars series:

Wish Upon a Superstar

by Phoebe Bright
illustrated by Karen Donnelly

SCHOLASTIC INC.

NEW YORK TORONTO LONDON AUCKLAND
SYDNEY MEXICO CITY NEW DELHI HONG KONG

With special thanks to Valerie Wilding

For Zack Littley

ISBN 978-0-545-42002-0

Text copyright © 2012 by Working Partners Limited
Cover art copyright © 2012 by Scholastic Inc.
Interior art copyright © 2012 by Karen Donnelly

12 11 10 9 8 7 6 5 4 3 2 1   12 13 14 15 16/0

Printed in China   68
First Scholastic printing, November 2012

Lucky Star that shines so bright,
Who will need your help tonight?
Light up the sky, and thanks to you
Wishes really do come true. . . .

Hello, friend!

I'm Stella Starkeeper, and I want to tell you a secret. Have you ever gazed up at the stars and thought that they could be full of magic? Well, you're right. Stars really are magical!

Their precious starlight allows me to fly down from the sky. I'm always on the lookout for boys and girls who are especially kind and helpful. I train them to become Lucky Stars — people who can make wishes come true!

So the next time you're under the twinkling night sky, look out for me. I'll be floating among the stars somewhere.

Give me a wave!

Love,

Stella Starkeeper

1

Strawberries and Sparkles

Cassie Cafferty was the only early-morning customer at Farmer Greg's "Pick Your Own" fruit farm. Hundreds of ripe red strawberries still dotted the lush plants, but her basket was full.

Cassie picked one last giant berry and popped it in her mouth. So juicy!

At the checkout, Farmer Greg said cheerily, "Hello, Cassie. Wow, you have enough strawberries here for everyone in Astral-on-Sea!"

"Mom's making strawberry shortcake as a treat for the guests at Starwatcher Towers," said Cassie.

"She must be awfully busy running the bed-and-breakfast every day," said Farmer Greg.

"You're right," said Cassie with a smile. She paid and took her basket. The scent from the sun-warmed fruit was sweet. "Mmmm!" she said. "The guests will love these. Thanks!"

Cassie walked along the edge of Whimsy Woods. There were a few dog walkers around, but otherwise she had the path to herself. She swung her basket cheerfully as she went, being careful not to drop any strawberries.

Suddenly, something in the woods caught Cassie's eye. She peered among the trees. Sunlight streaked the leaves, but farther in among the shadows, there was . . . yes! It was an orb of silver light, like a fallen star.

Cassie smiled. *Could that light be Stella Starkeeper?* she wondered. She hoped it was!

As Cassie pulled a branch aside, the

charms on her silver bracelet tinkled. Stella Starkeeper had given her the bracelet a few weeks ago, on her seventh birthday. But it was no ordinary charm bracelet. It held a magical secret!

Each charm on Cassie's bracelet gave her a special power. Whenever she helped make someone's wish come true, she received a new charm. Once she had all seven, she would become a Lucky Star! So far, Cassie had five charms. The little blue bird gave her the power to fly, and the crescent moon helped her talk to animals. With the pink butterfly she could stop time, and with the purple flower charm she could make things appear.

Cassie's newest charm was a cute cupcake,

but she and her friend Alex still hadn't figured out what power it had. Alex was the only other person who knew about the magical charms — aside from Stella, of course. He was staying at Starwatcher Towers for a few weeks with his parents and his puppy, Comet. He and Cassie had already become good friends!

Cassie watched the silver light dance farther into the trees.

"It's leaving!" she gasped. "I have to see if that really is Stella!"

She chased the light, but it moved too fast. Cassie realized that she needed the bracelet's magical power if she wanted to catch up. She concentrated hard on her bird charm.

Her wrist tingled! Sparkles swirled from her charm bracelet, then spiraled around her.

Cassie rose off the ground and flew after the light. She moved quickly through the trees, holding her basket of strawberries close so it wouldn't get caught on a branch.

The light darted along the deserted main path through Whimsy Woods. It was headed straight toward the town's outdoor movie theater!

* ✦ ★ ✳

Before long, Cassie reached the theater clearing. It was one of her favorite spots in Astral-on-Sea! A giant movie screen was set up on the far end. There were rows of benches to sit on, and a large grassy area where people could picnic. During movie screenings, snacks were sold at the kiosk that stood to one side.

Just then, Cassie spotted the silver light twinkling in front of a poster:

That looks interesting, thought Cassie, as she drifted gently to the ground.

Suddenly, the silver

Secrets of Astral on Sea

A special film showing this afternoon.

light burst into thousands of tiny sparkles that swirled toward her. With a *whizz* and a *fizz* and a *zip-zip-zip*, the sparkles gathered into a column of light.

Cassie's heart skipped a beat as the light changed into a beautiful woman. She held a wand that was tipped with a twinkling star, and all her clothes were silver. Star-shaped buttons glittered on the cuffs of her shiny jacket, and she wore a glistening crown.

The woman smiled and her velvety blue eyes twinkled.

"Hi, Stella!" cried Cassie, running to hug her.

"What a nice welcome," Stella said in her soft, warm voice. "And what pretty strawberries."

"Try them!" said Cassie, holding out her basket.

Stella chose a strawberry. "It's heart shaped!" she said. Then she tasted it. "Mmm, delicious!" She touched Cassie's bracelet with her wand. "You've earned five charms already."

Cassie nodded. "If I earn two more," she said, "I'll become a true Lucky Star, just like you."

"Yes, but until then, you must keep listening for someone to make a wish," said Stella. "When you become a Lucky Star, you won't need to wait—you'll be able to grant any wish you like, whenever you feel it's right." She smiled. "Do you like your new cupcake charm?"

"It's great," said Cassie, "but I don't know what power it has. Can you tell me?" she asked. "Or maybe give me a clue?"

Stella raised her wand above Cassie's head, and bright light shone down from it.

It seemed like Cassie was standing in a spotlight! She twirled like a ballerina. "Do I look like a star onstage?" she asked, laughing.

Stella smiled. "Not everybody enjoys being

in the spotlight, Cassie." She winked and popped another heart-shaped strawberry into her mouth. Then, with a wave of her wand, she vanished behind a veil of silvery sparkles.

As the sparkles drifted away, Cassie turned toward home, thinking about what Stella had said.

Not everybody enjoys being in the spotlight. . . .
Was that a clue?

2
Roxy Gold!

When Cassie came out of Whimsy Woods, she turned onto the road that went through Astral-on-Sea and along the beach. She glanced up at Starwatcher Towers, her cliff-top home, where she imagined Mom was busy getting ready to bake strawberry shortcake. She thought Dad might be in his observatory. He was an astronomer, and he was probably making notes about the stars he'd seen through his telescopes at night.

From here, Cassie could see that the sun glinted off the glass roof of her own cozy bedroom. She often lay on her bed and watched the stars through the glass. But her parents didn't know that she could also float up through the roof and fly among the stars with Stella!

Suddenly, Cassie heard a familiar noise. *"Errrgh-hee-errrgh-hee-errrgh!"*

It sounded like Bert's donkeys! But Cassie knew that they should be on the beach, giving rides to children. What could be going on?

Cassie hurried around the bend and saw Bert with three donkeys—in the middle of the road!

"Move, you silly animals," Bert was saying. "You're blocking the road."

Cassie giggled. Those donkeys could be difficult! "I'll help," she cried.

Bert wiped his forehead and looked up. "Thanks, Cassie," he said. "A speedboat came too close to the beach, and Coco got scared and ran off. Of course, the others followed." He tried to push a donkey out of the road, but the stubborn animal wouldn't move. "Lucky no one was riding them at the time."

"And lucky there are no cars around," said Cassie. She patted her favorite donkey. "Poor Coco, you're so jumpy. No wonder the speedboat frightened you." She held out a fat strawberry. "Here, would you like this?"

As Coco tried to nibble it, Cassie took a step backward. Coco followed, stretching for the strawberry. He was just about to step out of the road when a car came around the bend and glided to a stop. It couldn't go any farther, because the road was still blocked by the rest of the donkeys! The car was creamy white, with black windows, and it was very long.

Wow! A stretch limo, thought Cassie. *I wonder who's inside.*

Just then, Coco trotted back to his friends in the middle of the road.

"Oh, no!" groaned Bert, looking even more flustered than before.

Cassie felt sorry for him. "Don't worry," she said. "I'll explain everything to the driver. I'm sure he won't mind waiting a few minutes."

The limo driver smiled as Cassie walked up. But before Cassie could speak, the back window opened and a pretty girl looked out. She was a little older than Cassie, and wore a red top with sequined hearts on it, skinny jeans, high-heeled boots, and a red and gold necklace. Her glossy black hair tumbled over

her shoulders as she leaned forward, holding a pen and a photograph.

Cassie recognized her instantly. She was Roxy Gold, a famous movie star! Cassie couldn't believe it! She opened her mouth to say something, but she was so surprised that no words came out. What was Roxy Gold doing in Astral-on-Sea?

Roxy gazed dreamily at the beach for a moment. Then she looked at Cassie and flashed her famous smile.

"Who should I make it out to?" asked Roxy.

Cassie realized that Roxy thought she wanted an autograph, and felt herself blushing. "Oh, um, no . . ." she said. "I mean, yes, please, but . . . I really just wanted to explain about the donkeys."

"Donkeys?" said Roxy, leaning out the window to see. "Oh, aren't they sweet!" She turned to the man sitting next to her in the car. "Dad, let's go and help."

"That would be great," Cassie cried. "Thank you!"

Roxy opened the door. "Pete," she said to the driver, "can you wait here, please?"

Pete grinned. "Those donkeys aren't letting me go anywhere!"

Roxy laughed.

"I'll show you Coco," said Cassie. "He's my favorite."

Together, they all tried to coax the donkeys out of the road. But clicking their tongues, patting, and calling out made no difference.

A small crowd had started to gather nearby, staring at the limo. A little boy gasped. "Mom!" he shouted. "That's Roxy Gold!"

Cassie felt awfully important all of a sudden. People could see her, Cassie Cafferty, chatting with a superstar!

She wondered if anyone she knew was watching. To her delight, behind two wildly waving girls, she spotted a curly-haired boy with a fluffy white puppy and a big bag of library books.

"Hey, Alex!" she called to her friend.

He was hopping from foot to foot with excitement, pointing at Roxy

Cassie grinned and waved him over.

Alex's eyes widened. He slipped through the crowd and dropped his book bag on the side of the road. "Sit, Comet," he said.

The puppy leaned against

Cassie, wagging his tail madly.

Roxy was busy signing autographs. "Excuse me, Roxy," said Cassie. "This is my friend Alex. He's going to be a scientist."

"Hi, Alex," said Roxy. Then she noticed Comet. "Oh, you adorable ball of fluff!" she said, bending down and cuddling him. "Alex, you're so lucky. I can't have a puppy because I travel so much."

Alex went bright red. "Hi, Roxy," he said shyly. "I . . . I saw you in *Space Girl*. You were really great. And . . . um . . . and in *Tessa's Time Machine*, too."

"Thanks!" said Roxy. She looked so thrilled that Alex grinned the widest grin Cassie had ever seen! *Roxy must be super-famous if even Alex recognizes her*, she thought.

He's usually too wrapped up in his science experiments to pay much attention to movie stars.

Finally, after what seemed like forever, the donkeys decided to go back to the beach. But Roxy was still signing autographs, smiling brightly. Every now and then, she looked longingly back at the car.

"She must want to get going," Cassie

murmured to Alex. "I wonder if her hand hurts from signing so many autographs."

Alex just stared. "I can't believe Roxy Gold talked to me," he said. "And to Comet, too!"

Cassie smiled. "She's going to talk to us again," she whispered as Roxy walked toward them with her dad.

"We've heard about a really pretty B&B near here," said Roxy. "If there's room, we'd like to stay there for a while."

"It's called Starwatcher Towers," added

Roxy's dad. "Have you heard of it?"

Cassie and Alex grinned at each other, and Cassie was sure they'd both had the same exciting thought.

Roxy Gold is staying with us!

3
A Star at Starwatcher Towers

"Starwatcher Towers is my mom's B&B," said Cassie.

"Oh, fantastic!" said Roxy. "Could you show us how to get there?"

Cassie nodded. "Sure!"

Roxy opened the car door. "Jump in," she said. "You too, Alex. And you, cutie," she added to Comet, petting his fur.

Cassie sank into a scarlet leather seat next to Roxy and held her strawberry basket on her knees. Alex sat beside Cassie, and Comet settled on the deep red carpet.

Pete started the car. "Which way?" he asked.

"Take the beach road through town, then up the hill to the top of the cliff," said Cassie. She sat back and looked around the limo at the pretty lights and mirrors. "This is much more glamorous than how I usually get around—on a bike!" she said.

"I'd rather be riding a bike," said Roxy. "But the movie studios insist that I use the limo. They want me to act like a superstar all the time. Anyway," she added quietly, "I'm always so busy filming, I've never had time to learn how to ride a bike."

"Really?" said Cassie. She couldn't

believe it! "I'll teach you."

"Thanks!" said Roxy, her face lighting up. She opened a small door next to her seat. "Are you guys thirsty?"

Cassie gasped. "A fridge in a car!"

Roxy grinned. "And it's full of lemonade," she said. "Want one?" She passed drinks to Alex and her dad, too, who were busy talking about the car's different dials and switches and buttons.

As they sipped their lemonades, Roxy opened the window. "I love that ocean smell," she said.

Cassie giggled as Comet climbed onto Roxy's lap.

"He wants to sniff the ocean, too," said Roxy. She helped the puppy up so he could look out the window. "Ooh, look—the Fairy Cupcake Bakery!" She pointed to a building as they drove past.

"My friend Kate's mom runs the bakery," said Cassie. "And there's the Pier Theater, and Bert's cotton candy stall, and look—the fair's still here." She stopped. "I'm sure it's not as exciting as the places you're used to."

"Are you kidding? Astral-on-Sea looks great," said Roxy. "I've already discovered

★   ✳   ★   ✳

that it's a friendly place!"

The car headed uphill. Cassie gripped her
basket of strawberries as Alex's bag of books
fell off the seat. He gathered it up and pulled
out a crumpled pamphlet.

"What's that?"
asked Roxy.

Alex smoothed it
out. "It's from the
library," he said.
"A movie about
local legends is
being shown this
afternoon."

"Ooh, I saw a poster about that," said
Cassie. "It's at the outdoor movie theater in
Whimsy Woods."

"Whimsy Woods!" said Roxy. "That sounds like a magical place."

Alex looked at Roxy and his cheeks turned pink. Cassie could tell he was about to speak, but she knew how shy Alex was. *He'll never ask her*, she thought. So she said, "Roxy, would you like to come to the outdoor movie theater with us?"

"I'd love to," said Roxy with a big smile. "Thanks!"

As they reached Starwatcher Towers, Cassie's mom opened the front door. She watched Cassie climb out of the gleaming limo, followed by Alex and Comet.

"What in the world . . . ?" Mrs. Cafferty began in surprise, but she stopped as someone else emerged from the car.

Cassie laughed at her mom's amazed expression.

"You're Roxy Gold!" said Mrs. Cafferty, walking over to the limo. "Wow, welcome! Are you filming in Astral-on-Sea?"

Mr. Gold shook her hand. "I'm Roxy's dad," he said. "We're here for a quiet vacation, but we haven't booked a place to stay. We wondered if . . ."

"Oh, of course!" said Mrs. Cafferty. "I have some nice rooms available. Come in and join us for lunch!"

Mr. Gold followed her inside, but Roxy stopped and looked up at Starwatcher Towers.

"What's that funny round room up there?" she asked Cassie, pointing.

"My bedroom," Cassie said. "Come and see."

They ran upstairs, followed by Alex and Comet.

Roxy stared around the room. "I love your starry wallpaper," she said, "and the moon-shaped lamp." She looked up and gasped. "Wow! A glass ceiling!"

They heard Mom's voice call, "Lunch in five minutes!"

Cassie quickly showed Roxy to the room where she'd be staying.

"What a gorgeous view," said Roxy, peering out the window. "There's the beach and—look! Bert's donkeys, too! Oh, Cassie, I love it here already."

She opened her suitcase and pulled out

a denim skirt. "I'm going to change into something comfy."

"Okay, see you downstairs," said Cassie, turning to leave.

"*Mee-owwwww!*"

Cassie looked back over her shoulder. Twinkle, her black-and-white cat, must have been hiding under the bed. Now he was turning around in Roxy's suitcase, settling down right on top of her purple silk pajamas!

"Twinkle!" cried Cassie, embarrassed.

Roxy smiled. "It's okay, leave him there," she said. "He looks so cozy. But why is he meowing so much?" She went into the bathroom, giggling. "It's almost like he's talking to you."

He probably is! Cassie thought. When Roxy was out of sight, she concentrated on her crescent moon charm. Silver sparkles danced around her bracelet and swirled between her and Twinkle. Cassie knew the charm was giving her the power to understand animals.

Twinkle blinked his amber eyes. "She didn't throw me out," he said. "I like her, and I like it in this box thing."

Cassie blew him a kiss, then called out, "Roxy, Twinkle likes snuggling in your suitcase."

"Tell him I'm really glad that he likes it!" yelled Roxy.

Cassie whispered, "Twinkle, Roxy's happy, too."

"Well, of course," Twinkle purred. "I could make anyone happy."

Roxy appeared again, drying her face on a towel. She petted Twinkle gently. "Oh, Cassie," she said. "This is going to be the best vacation ever!"

4
An Accident

Cassie set some extra places at the table for lunch. Pete the limo driver was joining them, too, before bringing the limo back to the studio.

After they'd eaten salad and soup, Mrs. Cafferty brought out the strawberry shortcake and a blue jug full of thick cream. "Cassie picked the strawberries this morning," she said.

Cassie remembered giving Stella Starkeeper some strawberries at the outdoor movie theater. That made her think of Alex's pamphlet.

"Mom," she asked, "can we go to see *Secrets of Astral-on-Sea* at the Whimsy Woods theater this afternoon?"

"Of course," said Mom. "In fact . . ." She pulled an old book from the bookcase. "This is called *Astral-on-Sea Mysteries*." She flipped through the pages and showed everyone a picture of Whimsy Woods.

Roxy drew a sharp breath. "There are

golden lights shining in the trees!"

"Those are supposed to be the fairies of Whimsy Woods," said Mrs. Cafferty. "When I was younger, I used to look for them all the time. I never saw one, though."

"Me neither," said Cassie. *But I have seen a magical light among those trees!* she thought.

"The legend is well known," Mom went on. "I think secretly everyone would love to see a fairy."

Just then, two of the other B&B guests came into the dining room. The young couple stopped and stared in surprise when they saw who was at the table. Mrs. Cafferty held up some extra plates and said, "We have lots of strawberry shortcake left. Would you like some?"

But the couple said that they'd eat their shortcake out in the yard. "We don't want to intrude on Miss Gold," the woman said, smiling and waving as they headed outside.

When Pete left, Cassie's dad gave Mr. Gold a tour of his observatory. Alex helped Cassie clear the table, while Roxy went into the yard to chat with the guests.

"That's nice of her," Cassie said. "I'll bet they were dying to meet her, but they wanted to be polite." Then she whispered, "While we're out, I have to listen for someone making a wish. If I make it come true, I'll earn another charm."

Alex put the salt and pepper away. "I hope you do. I really want you to become a Lucky Star before my vacation is over." Comet

yipped and tilted his head to look up at Cassie with his big brown eyes. "So does Comet!" Alex laughed.

Cassie smiled, but she felt sad. Alex had become such a good friend. She couldn't imagine him not being around anymore! She was going to miss him and Comet so much when they had to leave.

"We need to take Comet for a walk before we go to the movie," said Alex.

"I have an idea!" said Cassie. "Let's invite Roxy to come for a walk with us. Then we can go to Whimsy Woods afterward."

Alex looked down at his feet. "Do you

think you could ask her?" he said shyly. "She's coming up the path now."

"Of course," said Cassie. She opened the kitchen door. "Roxy, we're going to walk Comet before we go to the movie. Want to come?"

"I'd love to!" Roxy replied.

Ten minutes later, Cassie, Alex, Roxy, and Comet wandered down to the beach. They waved to Bert and his donkeys, and Cassie called hello to Bert's son at the cotton candy booth.

Down at the pier, Roxy stopped. "Look! An ice cream stand," she said. "I'll buy you both an ice cream, as a thank-you for being so friendly."

"You don't need to do that!" said Cassie.

Roxy hesitated for a moment. "You do like me, don't you?" she asked quietly. "It's not just because I'm a movie star?"

Cassie looked at Alex with wide eyes, then said, "Are you kidding? We like you a lot! Not superstar Roxy, but our new friend Roxy. And we would definitely like some ice cream!"

Roxy grinned. "Will you go up and get them, Cassie?" she asked, handing Cassie some money.

Cassie looked at her, surprised.

"I might be recognized," Roxy explained, "and it's so nice just hanging out with you two."

"Okay," said Cassie. She hadn't thought of that!

While Cassie joined the ice cream line, Roxy waited with Alex and Comet. But when Comet barked excitedly, the ice cream man looked over at them.

"Hey!" he said. "You're Roxy Gold!" He called over to the woman in the burger van. "Look, Janice! It's Roxy Gold!"

Soon, Roxy was surrounded by people taking photos with their cell phones and asking for autographs.

Cassie felt sorry for her! Imagine getting all that attention, when Roxy just wanted to be a normal girl. She moved to Roxy's side. "Let's go down Main Street," she whispered. "Then we'll head for Whimsy Woods."

Alex carried Comet along Main Street, so he wouldn't accidentally trip people on the narrow sidewalks. They passed the Fairy Cupcake Bakery, and Cassie laughed when Kate's mom stared, openmouthed, at Roxy

through the window!

A little crowd had followed them, and more people joined along the way. They were all so excited to see a famous movie star.

Cassie showed Roxy the Flashley Manor Hotel, with its grand entrance and gold sign. "It's run by the parents of a girl I know, Donna Fox," she said. "As Donna's always saying, it's the fanciest hotel in town."

Suddenly, Cassie was jostled from behind and she stumbled. There were an awful lot of people following them now!

Roxy had a brave smile on her face, but the crowd was still growing.

A man with a large camera called, "Smile, Roxy!"

Cassie desperately tried to think how to help Roxy. If she used the flying charm, everyone would see. Talking to animals was no use. None of her charms were quite right. Maybe the cupcake charm could help—but how?

She stopped suddenly as Donna Fox appeared in front of her, scowling and crossing her arms.

"Got a new friend?" Donna asked Cassie. "Don't you know that superstars are supposed to stay at *our* hotel?"

Before Cassie could reply, a little girl ran toward them, waving a pen and notebook. But Roxy was signing an autograph and didn't notice.

The girl tugged at Roxy's sleeve. "Please, can I—" she began.

But she pulled so hard that Roxy tripped, and her foot slipped off the edge of the sidewalk. She fell right into the road.

"Ow!" she cried. "My knee!"

Quickly, Cassie and Alex helped Roxy to her feet.

Cassie was horrified. Her friend's leg was scraped and bleeding, and her face was white.

Poor Roxy!

5
Kara

"I'm sorry," the little girl whispered.

Roxy patted her shoulder. "It's okay, I'm fine," she said gently, but Cassie could see that her eyes were swimming with tears.

I have to find someplace quiet, Cassie thought. She guided Roxy toward the nearest store. Curtains covered the window and door, and a sign out front said *Grand Opening Tomorrow*. Even though the store seemed to be closed, Cassie could hear someone

moving inside. She knocked.

A woman with spiky pink hair opened the door. "What's wrong?" she asked.

"Please," said Cassie, "our friend scraped her knee. She just needs to sit quietly for a minute. Can we come in?"

"Of course," said the woman. She ushered

them inside and closed the door firmly. "My name's Kara."

Cassie ducked below a broom that hung from the ceiling. *That looks like a witch's broomstick*, she thought.

"I'm Cassie," she said. She gestured to her friends. "This is Alex, and this is . . ." Her voice trailed off. She knew that Roxy didn't want anyone else fussing over her.

"Don't worry," Kara said. "I recognize you, of course, Roxy, but I promise you'll have peace and quiet while you're here." She looked at Roxy's knee. "And a bandage, too! I'll go get one for you."

"Thank you, Kara," said Roxy. She managed a brave smile, then burst into tears.

Cassie shifted a heap of clothing from a

chair so Roxy could sit down. Before long, Kara returned with her first-aid box and began to clean Roxy's scraped knee.

"All I want is a quiet vacation," Roxy sobbed, "but wherever I go, there are always huge crowds. I can't be just me."

Cassie hugged her, finding it hard to believe that a famous movie star was crying on her shoulder.

"Oh, Cassie," Roxy sighed. "I wish I could go around unnoticed, just for one day. . . ."

Cassie froze, then looked at Alex. His eyes were wide.

Roxy made a wish! she thought. *I have to help make it come true. But how?* She touched her new cupcake charm, thinking. *I must be able to use this somehow. But what power does it have?*

Just then, Comet jumped up next to Roxy, gazing at her and giving her arm a sympathetic lick. On the chair beneath him Cassie noticed something that looked like a sparkly silver mermaid's tail.

A mermaid's tail? That's strange, she thought, looking around the shop for the first time.

Racks of clothes stood against the walls. There was a cowboy outfit, a ballerina's tutu, a scarecrow costume, and an astronaut's space suit—and lots more. She glanced down at the clothes she'd moved from the chair.

"A Captain Hook outfit!" she said. "And Peter Pan's hat . . . a giant rabbit suit . . ." She picked up something bright green and frizzy. "And a witch's wig!"

Kara smiled. "I'm opening a costume shop," she said. "These are costumes people will really notice!"

If Kara makes outfits that people notice, Cassie thought, *maybe I could make a costume that does the opposite—one that nobody notices at all.*

"Kara," she said, "could we please borrow some things? Just for the afternoon?"

Everyone looked confused.

"It's to help Roxy," Cassie added.

"Oh! Of course," said Kara, realizing what Cassie was planning.

Cassie looked through the racks of clothes and found a pair of baggy pants and a shirt decorated with palm trees. "Roxy, put these on."

"But . . ." Roxy began.

"If you wear a disguise, people won't recognize you," Cassie explained, passing her a pair of sandals. "It'll be like you're invisible."

Alex fished around in a box. "Try these, too," he said, passing Roxy some sunglasses. "We met a singer named Jacey Day, and she used dark glasses when she didn't want to be recognized."

Roxy closed the curtain on the doorway

of the changing room. When she reappeared in her new clothes, she did a twirl. "How do I look?" she asked, adjusting the sunglasses.

"Just a sec!" said Cassie, darting to the other side of the room.

She hunted through a cardboard box and pulled out a baseball hat. She put it on Roxy's head and tucked her long black hair inside.

"There!" Cassie said. "Now everyone will think you're just a tourist visiting the ocean for the day."

Alex laughed. "You look more like my cousin Suzie than Roxy Gold, movie star!"

Kara clapped her hands. "Amazing!" she said. "Look in the mirror."

Roxy smiled when she saw her reflection. "That's perfect!" she said. "Thank you, everyone. Let's try it out!"

Kara led them out of the back of the store and opened a door that led onto a side street. "All quiet," she said.

Roxy hugged Kara and said, "You've been so nice. Thanks for everything."

"We'll bring the clothes back tomorrow, Kara," said Cassie. "And we'd love to help with the grand opening — with Roxy in disguise, of course!"

Roxy held up crossed fingers. "Let's hope this works!"

Cassie crossed her fingers, too, wondering, *Will Roxy's disguise be enough to make her wish come true?*

6

Trouble in Whimsy Woods

As the friends approached Whimsy Woods, they joined groups of people. Everyone was heading along the path toward the outdoor movie theater.

"No one's recognized you so far," Cassie whispered.

"I know!" Roxy said happily, pushing the sunglasses farther up the bridge of her nose.

Just before the clearing was a chestnut tree with low branches. Cassie followed the other people as they ducked under. Roxy was next, then Alex.

Suddenly, Cassie heard Roxy cry out, "Oh, no!"

She turned around and saw that Roxy's hat had snagged on a tree branch, letting her black hair tumble free. As Cassie and Alex rushed to help Roxy put the hat back on, her sunglasses slipped off.

★ ✳ ★ ✳

"Look!" cried a girl nearby. "It's Roxy Gold!"

"Hey, Roxy!" the girl's friend called. "Can I have your autograph?"

"Me, too!" said a woman.

Roxy sighed, taking the pen and paper and giving a little smile.

"I'm sorry," Cassie said miserably.

"It's not your fault," said Roxy. She signed her name for the girls, and then for the woman. But now a line was forming behind them. Everyone wanted Roxy's autograph!

"Oh, if only I *was* invisible," Roxy mumbled quietly.

Cassie's bracelet jangled, reminding her of something Stella had said. What was it? *Not everybody enjoys being in the spotlight. . . .*

Hmm, she thought. *Roxy's so famous, it seems like she's always in the spotlight. But she doesn't want people to see her. . . .*

Suddenly, Cassie took Alex's arm and led him away from the crowd. Comet bounded after them.

"I think I know what kind of magic my cupcake charm gives me," Cassie said. "I think it has the power to make me invisible!"

"Really?" he said, raising his eyebrows. "Then you could make Roxy invisible!"

Cassie shook her head. "No. That would give away my secret. You're the only other person to know about it, and that's the way it has to stay."

"Why don't you experiment with the charm?" Alex suggested.

"Good idea," said Cassie.

They squeezed back through the crowd. Roxy was still signing autographs and posing for pictures, but her smile didn't make her eyes sparkle. She clearly wasn't having fun. *I need to do something fast*, Cassie thought.

"Roxy, would you watch Comet for a minute, please?" Cassie asked. "We'll be back soon."

"Sure," said Roxy, taking Comet's leash and giving the little puppy a cuddle. "It's a shame you can't sign your paw print, Comet."

Cassie led Alex behind an enormous oak tree. It had a thick trunk and lots of branches that hid them from sight. She gripped his hand and concentrated on her butterfly charm. Instantly, everyone and everything around them was still and silent. Cassie peered around the tree at Roxy, who was frozen to the spot with a pen in her hand.

Comet sat nearby on his hind legs, trying to lick her. The crowd around them was frozen to the spot, too.

"You stopped time!" Alex said excitedly.

Cassie nodded. "Now we have time to try out my new charm," she said.

Cassie let go of Alex's hand and concentrated on her cupcake charm. Silvery sparkles swirled around it. They danced in the air, then drifted to her fingertips and along her arm.

Alex gasped. "Your hand disappeared! Your arm's fading now!"

Cassie tingled all over as sparkles spun around her.

"I don't believe it!" Alex breathed, looking everywhere. "You're invisible!"

Cassie touched Alex's arm. Sparkles swirled around him, too.

"Wow!" he said. "Now *I'm* invisible!"

Cassie giggled. "I can hear you, but I can't see you."

Alex laughed in delight. "Let's hold hands in case we lose each other."

"But we'll need both hands free," said

Cassie. "I have an idea to distract everyone from poor Roxy. First, I'll use my flower charm to make something magical appear."

She held her wrist up, then gasped.

"My bracelet's invisible, too," she cried. "I can't see the charm!"

7
Fairies!

"What do we do now?" came Alex's voice from beside her left ear.

"Let me think," said Cassie. "Hey! That's it—I'll think, really hard. Maybe I don't have to actually *see* the charm for the magic to work."

Cassie pictured the flower charm in her mind and concentrated. She held her invisible hands out, palms up. *Think, Cassie*, she told herself.

Her palms tingled, and two glowing golden lights appeared before her. She moved her hands, and the lights moved, too.

"Did you create those lights?" asked Alex. "That's scientifically impossible."

"It's magic, not science," said Cassie. "Now touch my fingertips, but keep your palms up."

"Where are your fingers?" asked Alex.

"In front of the lights—that's it!" she said, as something brushed her thumb.

She felt Alex touching her fingertips and concentrated again.

"Whoa!" said Alex as two more golden lights appeared in his hands. "They feel like fluttering butterflies."

"Fairies, not butterflies," said Cassie with

a grin. "Remember my mom said that the Whimsy Woods fairies looked like little lights? We'll bring the legend to life! Follow me, and do what I do. Oh!" she said. "I almost forgot."

She closed her eyes and pictured her butterfly charm. Whirling sparkles appeared. Instantly, everything and everyone in Whimsy Woods came to life again! Cassie heard the crowd around Roxy calling out her name and saw them snapping more photos. Comet licked Roxy, making her laugh as she patiently signed autographs.

Still invisible, Cassie slipped through the shadowy trees, moving her hands and the glowing lights around in the air. She saw Alex's lights moving nearby. But four tiny lights didn't exactly make Whimsy Woods look like it was filled with fairies.

Just then, Cassie glimpsed something bright over to the left. Another light! And another on the right! And another! Soon Whimsy Woods was full of dancing lights, twinkling like tiny golden stars.

Cassie guessed who had created the lights. "Thank you, Stella Starkeeper," she whispered.

Suddenly, someone shouted, "Look! Whimsy Woods fairies!"

People began calling to one another, "Fairies! Come and see!"

The crowd drifted away from Roxy and followed the dancing lights, gazing in wonder at the magical sight.

Cassie found Alex's hand. She pictured the cupcake charm in her mind. Sparkles swirled, and they could see each other again.

They found Roxy in the clearing, with Comet snuggled in her arms. "Aren't the fairy lights beautiful?" she asked, smiling. "And look—everyone's gone after them and left me alone!"

"They'll be back soon," Cassie warned. She helped Roxy put her baseball hat on again.

"Quick!" said Alex.

The twinkling lights were fading, and people were heading back, chattering excitedly. They'd forgotten all about Roxy.

The three friends settled on a bench in the clearing.

"By the way, where did you disappear to?" Roxy asked.

"Oh, the movie's starting!" Cassie said. She caught Alex's eye and winked.

★ ★ ★

After the movie, the three friends set off along the woodland path.

"That was amazing!" said Roxy. "I've learned so many cool things about Astral-on-Sea, and this is only my first day here."

"It was great," said Cassie. "I loved how everyone cheered at the part about the fairies!"

"What a great idea to have fairies in the woods first," said Roxy. "Fantastic special effects!"

Cassie and Alex both smiled.

★ ✳ ★ ✳

"And they made everyone leave you alone," said Cassie.

Roxy frowned. "I shouldn't grumble," she said. "I love acting, and I won't always be famous. Soon people will find something else more exciting!"

"Like fairies!" Alex laughed. "But you're so popular," he added, blushing, "you'll be famous for years."

"I'd love to be famous for a day," Cassie said. "It must be so exciting."

Roxy grinned. "It is exciting," she said, "but it's also nice to have this one afternoon of not being recognized. Now," she added, "what disguises should we wear for Kara's grand opening tomorrow?"

"I might be the astronaut," said Alex.

"Should I be the witch, with a terrible green face?" asked Roxy.

"I think I'll be a movie star for a day!" Cassie piped up with a grin.

They all collapsed into giggles.

"You'll need another disguise for learning to ride my bike," Cassie told Roxy.

Roxy smiled happily. "It's going to be a wonderful vacation in Astral-on-Sea," she said. "Thanks to you, I can just be . . . me!"

Cassie's wrist tingled.

She paused to glance at her
bracelet while the others went
on ahead. A glittering heart-
shaped charm dangled from it, and silver
sparkles drifted on the breeze.

Cassie smiled to herself. She had to make
just one more wish come true, then she would
become a true Lucky Star!

How exciting! But she couldn't help
worrying a little. Alex had been with her
through all of her magical adventures. . . .

*Can I become a Lucky Star before he has to
leave?*

She sure hoped so!

Make Your Own!

Roxy Gold is a glamorous superstar — and you can be, too! Decorate a pair of sunglasses to make your very own superstar shades.

You Need:
- A pair of oversized dark sunglasses (Make sure your parents don't mind!)
- Craft glue
- Sequins, rhinestones, and any other fun embellishments you like

Use the glue to attach your sequins, rhinestones, and other decorations to the sunglass frames, all the way around. Once dry, put on your fabulous sunglasses and strike a pose. You look like a true superstar!

Can Cassie make one more wish come true,
and become a real Lucky Star?
Take a special sneak peek at

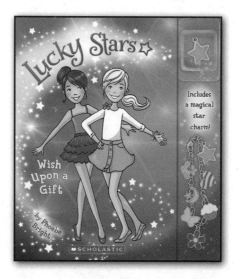

#6: Wish Upon a Gift!

1
Crystal Gifts

Cassie looked at her friend Alex's suitcase and frowned. It was overflowing with beach toys, shells, and brightly colored rocks. Alex picked up his microscope and tried to squeeze it in.

"It won't fit," he groaned.

"Here's one more thing for you to pack," Cassie said.

She held out a photo album with *Alex's Vacation* written on the front. For the last two weeks, Alex and his family had been staying at Starwatcher Towers, the bed-and-breakfast run by Cassie's parents. But now his vacation was over.

"The album's full of good memories," she said, trying to smile.

Alex nodded and cleared his throat. He smiled back, but Cassie could tell he was sad. Even Comet, his little white puppy, had his ears down.

Alex opened the album and laughed. There was a picture of Comet chasing a ball with Twinkle, Cassie's old cat.

"They're such good friends," Cassie said.

"Just like us," Alex replied. "I wished for a friend—and you became my best friend ever!"

"Your wish was the first one I helped come

true," Cassie said. "And you're the only person who knows about my magic charms."

They both looked down at Cassie's pretty charm bracelet. So far, she had six charms that each gave her a magical power! The bird gave her the power to fly, the crescent moon allowed her to talk to animals, the butterfly let her stop time, the flower made things appear, and the cupcake charm gave her the power to become invisible. *I still need to find out what power my new heart charm gives me, though*, Cassie thought.

"You only need one more charm," said Alex. "Then you'll be a Lucky Star, and you can make wishes come true anytime you want!"

Cassie sighed. "If only you could stay and help me."